REVIEWS OF

MILO AND ONE DEAD ANGRY DRUID

...ipping stuff for age eight-plus and its lively style
...kes it a good bet with reluctant readers.

Evening Echo

...illiantly written with clever humour and twists
...d turns.

Woman's Way

...citing supernatural adventure ... great humour,
...ce and cliffhangers that will keep young readers
...rning the pages and looking forward to more in
...e series.

Children's Books Ireland Recommended Reads Guide 2013

Mary Arrigan studied at the National College of Art, Dublin, and at Florence University. She became a fulltime writer in 1994. Her novel for teenagers, *The Rabbit Girl*, one of her forty-two published books, was selected by The United States Board of Books for Young People on their list of Outstanding International Books for 2012. Her awards include the International White Ravens title, a Bisto Merit Award, *The Sunday Times* Crime Writers Association Award and The Hennessy Short Story Award. Her books have been translated into twelve languages. You can read more Milo Adventures in *Milo and One Dead Angry Druid*, and *Milo and the Long Lost Warriors*.

THE MILO ADVENTURES

MILO AND THE RAGING CHIEFTAINS

WRITTEN AND ILLUSTRATED BY
MARY ARRIGAN

THE O'BRIEN PRESS
DUBLIN

First published 2014 by The O'Brien Press Ltd.,

12 Terenure Road East, Rathgar, Dublin 6, Ireland.

Tel: +353 1 4923333; Fax: +353 1 4922777

E-mail: books@obrien.ie

Website: www.obrien.ie

ISBN: 978-1-84717-561-8

10 9 8 7 6 5 4 3 2 1

18 17 16 15 14

Layout and design: The O'Brien Press Ltd.

Cover illustrations: Neil Price

Printed and bound by CPI Group (UK) Ltd, Croydon, CR0 4YY

The paper in this book is produced using pulp from
managed forests.

The O'Brien Press receives assistance from

For Emmett and Liz with thanks for all the sunshine and fun

CONTENTS

CHAPTER ONE

A VISIT TO THE CASTLE

'There's going to be cakes, Milo,' my pal Shane said. 'Loads of cakes.'

We were passing the castle on our way home from football training. Well, sort of training – Shane and I spend most of the time as far from the ball as possible. Not that we're wimpy cowards, it's just that both of us are big into the skills of self-preservation. Shane has a book about all that. It's mostly about how to save yourself from falling rocks, wild hairy creatures with fangs, and slimy things that spit slop in your eye. It was Shane who pointed out to me that most of the guys on the football field have all of those skills, but not us. So we're very good at looking like we're moving about a lot on the pitch.

'Cakes, Milo,' Shane went on.

'What about cakes?' I asked. 'Can you not go five minutes without thinking of food?'

'At the opening of the castle in two days' time.' He was already rubbing his fat tum at the thought. 'There'll be all sorts of food *for free*. Gran has made loads of African bikkies and stuff.'

Shane lives with his gran, Big Ella, who brought dozens of exotic African recipes with her when she and Shane came to live here, so there were always great smells floating from their house.

'What else is better than food?' asked Shane. 'Hey, look,' he stopped and pulled me back. 'That gate,' he whispered.

Sure enough one of the huge gates, covered with boards to stop people gawking in, was slightly open. For over two years the castle had been shut off from the public while it was being done up. Nobody had been allowed in except the men with hard yellow hats and the beardy experts who shuffled in every day with rolled-up charts under their arms. Sometimes we could see them high up on the battlements, looking at the charts and doing a lot of pointing around the castle grounds.

'Look at them up there,' Shane said to me once. 'Gargoyles in anoraks.'

Which was a spot-on observation.

'Hey, Milo,' Shane whispered. 'Let's sneak in and have a look, eh?'

'Shane, those guys would probably shove us into a dungeon for trespassing. Can't you see the KEEP OUT signs plastered all over the place?'

'Oh, come on, Milo,' laughed Shane. 'Just a quick look and we'll scarper. Then we can boast about it at school and get serious respect.'

It was the word 'respect' that won me over. I once watched an old gangster movie with Dad, and I especially remember the part where the head gangster shook hands with someone who used the word 'respect', and I thought I'd like people to greet me like that. Not as a gangster, though. Dad is a Garda and he says the food is pretty sloppy and the place is ice cold. 'And that's just the Garda Stations, son,' he'd added. 'So you can imagine what the cells are like for crooks and gangsters.'

Still, I was just as curious as Shane.

'Alright,' I said. 'Just a quick look.'

'I knew you'd say that,' Shane said, laughing.

CHAPTER TWO

SHANE SHOWS OFF

We slipped in through the partly open gate and stayed near the wall.

'Wow!' we both said together. Where there had been crumbling stones and piles of rubbish, there was now a big cobbled courtyard that stretched all around the castle. The castle itself was like something in a historical movie. You know the kind of thing – guys with swords and armour and helmets that had long bits squashing their noses. Shane said that was to stop snot from dripping on the chest armour and making it rusty. The stone walls had been cleaned and the big windows had glass in them. Over the huge arch there was a sort of balcony thing.

'I know what that is,' said Shane. 'It has no floor, just openings.'

'Yeah?' I sniggered. 'A sort of outdoor loo? What if someone comes knocking at the door underneath and they get covered in wee and ...?'

'Don't be such a wuss,' said Shane. 'Nothing so ordinary.'

'How do you know all this stuff?' I asked.

'Gran buys old books about Ireland in the charity shop. She wants us to know all about this side of the world.'

Shane and his gran, Big Ella, had come to live here when he was little. He's my best mate. Big Ella spends most of her time painting huge colourful pictures. Her most famous one, 'The Druidstone', is hanging in the town museum.

'We read one about castles in olden times,' Shane was saying.

'What?' I said.

'You're not listening, dopey Milo.'

'I am. Go on.'

'Well, really listen. What's the point in me having to read heavy stuff if you don't listen? I'm telling you that the people in castles like this used to pour oil from that place up there on to enemies down here who'd try to break in the big door.'

'For real?' I said. 'Cool.'

'Not cool, Milo,' laughed Shane. 'Hot, actually.'

'What do you mean?' I asked.

'The oil would be boiling hot, Milo.'

'Awesome!' I gasped.

'Not so awesome if it was just a few neighbours coming for tea and bikkies, and a daft sentry up there thinking they were enemies. Imagine that, Milo.'

'Hey,' I grinned. 'Then the word "hothead" would have real meaning, wouldn't it?'

'That's gross,' said Shane, giving me a push that made me drop my bag of football gear. I shoved it behind a rock so that I wouldn't have to haul it with me while we sneaked around. We could hear the hammering from the courtyard as we eased our way along by the boundary wall.

'Good job your face is dark and your sweatshirt is *grey*, Shane,' I said. 'They fit in with the stone wall so you won't be seen. I'll stand on the inside and hide behind you,

17

so that I won't be seen either.'

'What do you mean my sweatshirt is *grey*?' he said. 'It's white, just like yours.'

I put my sleeve against his. 'See?' I said.

'Doh! You're right,' he nodded his head. 'Gran just shoves all colours into the washing machine. She doesn't do like it says in the ads on telly.'

'Listen to us, Shane,' I said, grinning. 'We're trespassing here, in an ancient historic castle where we could be caught and dumped in a dungeon, and we're talking like a couple of sissies in a soap ad!'

We laughed at that.

When we made it around to the front of the castle, we stopped dead, too gobsmacked for words.

The main entrance to the castle that had been boarded up for years and years – even before Mum and Dad had been born – was totally done up.

'That's more than awesome,' I whispered. 'They've even restored the portcullis.'

'The what?' Shane whispered back.

'The portcullis,' I explained. Ha, I was glad that I knew something he didn't. I have a Lego fort in my bedroom that I play with. Just now and then, only when I'm really bored, of course. 'That huge pointy gate thing up there,' I said. 'That would be lowered during a battle to stop attackers getting in from the front.'

'And what about the boiling oil around the other side?' asked Shane.

'Well, I suppose they only used that if some gang actually did get in the back way,' I said lamely.

There was a shout from under the portcullis and two men headed towards us. And they were angry.

We made it to the back gate and out on to the pavement, still running until we reached an alley off the street. We both leaned against the wall and heaved breath into our lungs.

Then we heard voices that we very definitely didn't want to hear.

CHAPTER THREE

MISS LEE TO THE RESCUE

'**W**ell, well, if it isn't the dozy duo. Is the bogey man after you, guys?'

It was our arch enemies, Wedge and Crunch, two toughs always up to no good.

'What scared you nerds?' sneered Wedge.

'Scared? Nah,' I said, trying to sound tough and confident – but the words sounded like a sick mouse coughing up a bit of hard cheese.

Crunch grabbed my jacket and pulled me so close to his ugly face that I could see right up his nose. Not a pretty picture, I tell you.

'Hello, boys.'

We all turned. I was never so glad to see a teacher, especially when it was our own class teacher, Miss Lee, her shiny red, high-heeled shoes clip-clopping as she came towards us.

'Having a nice chat, are we?' she went on, her eyes boring holes into Wedge and Crunch.

'Just chatting to the lads here, Miss,' said Wedge, all smarmy.

'Yeah, chattin',' added Crunch, letting go of my jacket and pretending he was just brushing it down. 'About school,' he sniggered.

'Ah, that's great,' said Miss Lee. 'I love

chatting about school. Can I join your discussion, boys? What do you like best about school? Do tell.'

Wedge's head shrank between his shoulders. He looked at his wrist where a watch might have been but wasn't.

'Erm ... we have to be somewhere in a minute, me and Crunch,' he muttered.

'Go where, Wedge ...?' Crunch began, before Wedge gave him a dig on the shoulder.

'Oh, do you really have to go, lads?' asked Miss Lee. 'Shame. Catch you some other time for that chat then.'

They scarpered down the road. Wedge stopped for a second to look back with a warning glare at me and Shane. We moved closer to Miss Lee. To protect her, you understand.

'Well, you two,' she said. 'Did you enjoy your tour?'

'What do you mean, Miss?' asked Shane, all wide-eyed innocence.

'I mean that I was inside the castle and saw you two trespassers skulking about. Luckily, I was chatting with one of the people working on the restoration, and told him you were harmless. If I knew you were interested, I could have shown you around. My ancestors—'

'Harmless!' I interrupted. I'd have preferred to be called a hooligan or something a bit more macho.

Shane's belly wobbled as he thumped his chest. 'Oh, Miss,' he said. 'We're tough me and Milo. If you hadn't come along, we'd have knocked those two into pulp and left them on the ground for stray dogs to eat ...'

'Of course you would, Shane,' chuckled Miss Lee. 'Now, get along home both of you. Next time I might not be here to save you from bullies and raging workmen.'

'Whew,' I said to Shane as we ran home. 'That was a close shave.'

'No way,' he panted. 'We really would have flattened those two poo-bags.'

'Shane,' I laughed. 'We'd be dragging our way home carrying our heads in our hands if Miss Lee hadn't come along.'

'Yeah,' he said sheepishly as we came to our road. 'Maybe.'

As he threw his kitbag over the gate to his house, my heart did a double somersault.

'Oh, shoot!' I cried out.

'What's up?' Shane asked, climbing over the gate like he always does, because he's too lazy to use the bolt that's gone stiff.

'My football kit!' I yelped. 'I've left it in the castle courtyard! Mum will explode!'

'You'd better get moving, then,' said Shane, looking at his watch. 'The castle will be locked in five minutes.'

I was stunned. My best mate turning his back on me and walking away!

'Shane!' I yelled. 'Come on. You can't leave me in this mess.'

He turned around and grinned. 'I'm getting my bike,' he said. 'You go and get yours. We'll never make it in time on foot.'

'I can't,' I said. 'Mum would see me and ask questions.'

'That's OK, Milo,' said Shane. 'You can ride passenger on mine.'

'Your new bike?' I exclaimed. 'Cool.'

Now that's real friendship. Big Ella had bought Shane a super bike for his birthday. But just as my heart began to switch to a normal beat, the front door opened and Big Ella pranced out, eyes blazing.

'Shane!' she boomed. 'What time do you call this? You should have been home an hour ago.'

Shane's face wobbled. 'Milo and me, we were just—' he began.

'I don't care where you two were just. You get in here now before your dinner shrivels to soot. And Milo,' she added, turning her eyes on me, 'you'd best get home too, boy. Your mum's been looking for you.'

We exchanged defeated glances. You don't argue with Big Ella when she rants.

'You can tell your mum that I have your football kit,' Shane muttered. 'We'll get it tomorrow. Don't worry.'

'If it's still there,' I groaned.

Mum wasn't home when I let myself in. She had left a note to say that she'd gone to pick up Dad because the Garda car had a puncture. My heart sank when I saw the basket of dirty clothes beside the washing machine. I knew she'd ask me for my football kit to put in with them. I took a deep breath and resigned myself to what I had to do. Maybe if I cycled to the castle, I might be just in time to slip through that gate. The word 'maybe' is not very comforting when you're in a serious fix.

CHAPTER FOUR

AN OLD FRIEND RETURNS

I raced through the town, keeping a watchful eye for Mum and Dad in the oncoming traffic and trying to make up a reason why I was belting along the street on my bike. I couldn't believe my luck when I got to the back gate of the castle and found that it still hadn't been bolted properly. I just about managed to squeeze my bike in and headed for the place where I'd left my kit. The silence was the first thing I noticed. No hammering or voices. And the sinking sun was making the dark corners and arches mighty creepy in the big, silent courtyard. I wheeled my bike over to the place where I'd hidden my football kit. There it was! 'I'm saved,' I said out loud, securing the kitbag on the carrier and mounting the bike. Mission accomplished. 'Yee ha!' I whooped. That's when I heard another voice from above.

'Ah, Milo, my friend.'

Sitting high up in the arch of a window was a face and shape I knew well.

'Mister Lewis!' I shouted. 'It's you! I can't believe it.'

Sure enough, it really was my good, dead friend who'd helped me save Shane and Big Ella from the clutches of an ancient angry druid called Amergin.

'The same old me,' he replied. 'I was hoping to meet you.'

'I thought you'd be kinda wafting on clouds and, eh, looking a bit more ...'

'A bit more stylish and handsome?' he put in.

'Something like that,' I said, looking at the same old shabby coat and leaning-to-one-side high hat. 'Not wishing to hurt your feelings or anything, but I'd have thought you'd at least have a decent suit and a harp.'

'Harp parp!' he said with a sniff. 'Hmff. No such luck. I'm in a sort of holding place.'

'A what?' I asked.

'It's where dead people like me are sent to help others who've made mistakes in life to go back and sort things out.'

'So, who are you helping?' I asked, looking warily around the deserted courtyard. Mister Lewis leaned back towards the window.

'It's all right,' he called out. 'Milo is my very good friend. You can come out now.'

I was still wary of seeing any more deceased ancients shuffling about. I steeled myself for whatever big ghoul would appear. No fears, I told myself – fearfully. Mister Lewis will protect me. Still, I picked up my bike, ready for a quick exit.

I looked up at the window where Mister Lewis was holding out his hand behind him to help out whatever was in there. The first thing that appeared on the parapet was a skinny leg followed by another skinny leg, both of them in red tights. So far so unscary. The rest followed – a red, silky sort of frock, a pale face, sticky-out ears and a head of long, spiky red hair, down to the shoulders.

'A girl!' I shouted up to Mister Lewis. 'You've been lumbered with helping a skinny girl!' I had to laugh.

Mister Lewis shook his head – slowly in case an ear or part of his nose might drop off.

The figure stood up straight on the parapet, hands on hips, eyes glaring down at me.

'Ossie,' said Mister Lewis. 'Take that scowl off your face and say hello to my good friend, Milo ...'

'Osgur,' the redhead interrupted. 'My name is Osgur, in honour of my father's ancestor.'

'I know, I know,' said Mister Lewis. 'So you keep telling me.'

I was surprised at his attitude.

'You shouldn't be rude to a girl, Mister Lewis,' I called up.

'I'm not a girl. I'm a BOY!' Ossie shouted down at me.

Well, there was no answer to that. Folks from the past have strange taste in clothes and hairstyles, that's for sure. However, I didn't fancy hanging about listening to a grumpy guy, especially one in a frock.

'I'd best be off home, Mister Lewis,' I said. 'It's great to see you again, but it's getting dark. I'll be in right trouble ...'

'No, Milo. Wait!' Mister Lewis called out. 'We need your help. Can you come back tomorrow night? About ten thirty would be good.'

'Huh?' I exclaimed.

'Please,' Mister Lewis added urgently.

'How could *I* help?' I began. 'What would—?'

'Good lad. I knew we could depend on you,' Mister Lewis interrupted, before I could find a polite way to say 'no' to more ghostly shenanigans.

'Oh, and bring your bicycle,' he added, before the two of them disappeared inside.

CHAPTER FIVE

DAD'S ADVICE

Luckily, I got home just minutes before Mum and Dad arrived.

'Sorry we're late, Milo,' said Mum. 'We met your nice Miss Lee in the supermarket and we went for coffee.'

'She says you're a great kid,' said Dad.

'No need to sound so surprised, Dad,' I muttered.

'Surprised? No,' he said, straight-faced. 'Just shocked.'

I wondered how really shocked he'd be if I told him I'd been at the castle talking to a couple of ghosts. I should have said 'no' to Mr Lewis. And now he'd gone away thinking I would meet him the next night. I was so worried I stayed up as late as possible. I even offered to make sandwiches for Mum and Dad to stretch out the time, but they just fell about laughing and sent me to bed.

'You might be sorry' was my parting shot. As I went upstairs, I imagined them sniffling into their hankies and being totally woebegone when me and my bike disappeared. That would teach them a lesson – except I wouldn't be around to say 'I told you so'. I'd be floating about on cold moonlit nights.

When Dad arrived in my room later with a mug of hot chocolate, I was still sifting through all the scariest stuff you could imagine.

'I thought you were looking a bit peaky, son,' he said, sitting on the bed and feeling my forehead. 'Everything OK?'

'No, Dad,' I sighed. 'I've kinda promised to help someone and now I don't want to.'

'Well,' he said, 'do what I do when I don't want to face up to a big guy with a squashed face and a hammer who's running out of a shop with wads of cash.'

'You run away,' I said eagerly. 'That's the right thing to do, isn't it? Save yourself.'

'No, lad.' Dad was shaking his head. 'I do what a cop is supposed to do. I nab him because I've sworn to do that. And that's how it is. If you've promised help, then it's only right to go through with it. You want to talk about it?'

'No thanks, Dad,' I whispered, so that my

voice wouldn't come out as a scream. If I told him the truth, my dad would laugh and pat my head before sending me to a shrink, who'd be even scarier than any of the dead people I've come up against.

'OK,' said Dad, getting up. 'You'll be glad when you've helped. You're an honourable kid, Milo,' he went on as he plumped my pillow. 'Now, get that hot choc inside you and get some sleep. You'll laugh at yourself in the morning.'

'Yeah, Dad, I'm laughing already,' I groaned.

CHAPTER SIX

WHERE'S MISS LEE?

Naturally, after a night of tossing about before finally falling asleep when the town clock chimed three a.m., I was late for school. The shouting was the first thing that stopped me in my tracks. It was coming from my classroom! Then I figured Miss Lee was putting on some sort of modern play – she often does kooky things like that.

Everyone was jumping around like mad fleas. Of course they all stopped dead when I came in.

'Aw, it's only Milo,' Willy Jones shouted and they all went back to yelling and chasing.

'What's up?' I asked Shane.

'Miss Lee isn't in,' he said, offering me a bite of his lunch apple.

'Not in? Miss Lee not in?'

'Yep,' he went on. 'And her car isn't outside. She's been abducted by aliens,' he cried.

'That's a hairy old joke, you nerd,' I said.

The word 'hairy' was scarcely out of my mouth when the door opened and the principal stormed in.

'And there's another hairy old joke,' Shane giggled in my ear, before I slipped into my own desk.

Everyone stopped.

'You hooligans!' she bellowed. 'I could

hear you from my office. Miss Lee is – eh – not available, so I'll be with you for the rest of the day.'

We would all have groaned out loud, but we were too distracted, not so much by Miss Lee being absent, but by our constant fascination with the wobbly hairs above the principal's upper lip.

Every now and then someone would come to the door, and the principal talked to them in whispers. She looked so worried that she never even asked us to hand up the yawny stuff she gave us to write. It got so that we didn't even bother to try out the sums or puzzles she dished out on the whiteboard. Instead, we drew mad cartoons and passed them around. And she never even noticed when we sniggered.

'Do you think Miss Lee has done a runner?' Shane asked me on the way home.

'I know I would if I had to teach our class.'

'Shane,' I said, laughing. 'It's no big deal. My mum says that teaching is such a stressful job that teachers should be able to take the odd day off, to stop them from going mad. Miss Lee is probably at home with her feet up, munching chocolate and watching daytime telly.'

'Cool,' said Shane. 'I think I'll go for teaching instead of nuclear psychics.'

'Physics, you nelly,' I said. 'Come on, let's get our bikes.'

It was only when I went home to our empty house (Mum works in a home for the elderly two afternoons a week) that my mind threw up the whole Mister Lewis thing. I had pushed it to the back of my head all day, but now it was back like a giant wart sitting on my nose. How would I get myself out of this mess?

'Are you ready?' Shane appeared at my door and his loud bellow broke my thinking. 'So, where will we go?' he asked, fastening the shiny red helmet he'd got to match his bike. He was wearing his new rapper T-shirt. 'Somewhere out of town?'

'Sure,' I agreed, putting on my own blue helmet. Anything to avoid thinking about Mister Lewis and our meeting.

'What about down by the castle and out the road beyond that?'

I shivered. That 'castle' word almost caused me to fall down.

'NO!' I shouted too loudly. 'I don't want to go there.'

'Why not? You're always going on about the castle.'

I looked at his beaming face, and I so wanted to tell him everything, but even Shane wouldn't believe me. He was bound to double up laughing and make me feel even worse. 'Maybe go in the opposite direction,' I went on more calmly. 'Let's go the old road to the ruined cottages.'

'OK,' said Shane. 'The old road will be fine.'

That's what's great about having a pal like Shane. He doesn't go fussy when things don't go his way.

CHAPTER SEVEN

A FIND ON THE ROCKS

More than a hundred years ago there had been cottages along the old road, but when the people left for America, or some other place with paid work and sunshine, the cottages fell into ruins.

'Wow,' said Shane. 'Look at all that grass. Acres and acres of it. Gran says that there are huge areas in Africa where there's no grass at all. Imagine that, Milo. Baldy fields.'

We left our bikes on the ground and wandered into the ruined cottages. Some of them even had broken chairs and rusty kettles and things like that, just left there.

'Why did they leave their stuff?' Shane muttered, picking up a dinged tin cup and shaking his head.

'I suppose they were rushing away to catch the ship,' I said. 'Wouldn't you do a runner too if you were living in this misery? Anyway, this is boring. Let's go a bit farther.'

We wandered along beyond the cottages and into a wilderness of weeds and half-hidden stones. It was Shane who found the first carving.

'Hey, Milo,' he called out. 'You have to see this.'

'What have you found?' I laughed. 'A dozy leprechaun?'

'Don't be so dumb,' said Shane. 'Look.' He pointed to a stone in the grass. 'That looks like part of an arch.'

We gave it a closer look. Sure enough, it *was* part of an arch with carvings on it.

'Did the people who used to live in these cottages make things in stone, Milo?'

'I wouldn't think so,' I said. 'Their whole time was spent catching things to eat and knitting woolly jumpers. Anyway carvings like that were way before these cottages.'

'Let's see if we can find any more arches,' said Shane, moving away.

'Boring,' I groaned. But I followed him. Sure enough, the farther on we went, the more we found lots of fragments of carved stones.

'Maybe when they were building the town castle,' Shane went on, 'these were the ones that were rejects, like carvers made mistakes and had to dump them, because you can't rub out mistakes on stones like when you're drawing.'

'Good thinking,' I said, looking around. 'Look there's loads of them all over the place, hidden in the grass.'

'Or maybe a World War II bomb fell here,' whispered Shane, looking up at the sky. 'KABOOM! And the whole place fell apart.'

'Nah,' I said. 'The Germans didn't bomb small places like this, in the middle of nowhere.'

'It's kinda spooky, isn't it?' said Shane, looking around the wasteland.

That brought up all the fears I'd been holding back. I gave a huge sigh and sank on to the grass, covering my face with my hands.

'I wish we could rub out bad days, Shane,'

I sighed.

He laughed and threw some grass at me. 'You daft nutter,' he said. 'Hey,' he went on, when I still had my hands over my face. 'What's up, man?'

'I have to go somewhere tonight,' I squeaked.

'Ha. That's it?' Shane laughed. 'What's so awful about that?'

I looked at my best friend, and I so needed tell him everything, but something in the grass caught his attention.

'Hey!' he shouted, looking over my shoulder. 'Doesn't Miss Lee wear shoes like that?'

'She does!' I exclaimed, looking at the shoes tucked neatly beside a broken carving in the grass. There was no mistaking the red high heels and the shiny little half moons on the toes.

CHAPTER EIGHT

WEDGE AND CRUNCH

'**W**hat will we do with them, Milo?' Shane asked.

'We'll hold on to them,' I said.

'Not me!' Shane backed away. 'Fingerprints, Milo. We'd be interrogated and jailed for theft.'

'How did they get here?' I whispered. 'Surely Miss Lee didn't come all the way here on her own and lose her shoes?'

'That's it!' yelled Shane. 'She's been kidnapped or, maybe ...' He put his hands around his throat and gurgled loudly.

'That's ultra gross,' I said.

'Or,' Shane's imagination was working overtime, 'she might have been looking for rare rocks, or flowers, or something, and fell and banged her head and is wandering around with concussion.'

'And left her shoes here, all neat and tidy?' I scoffed. 'I'm going to search for her,' I went on, putting the shoes inside my jacket and zipping up.

'Me too,' Shane said.

We wandered around, tripping over more and more broken stones and carvings buried in the grass. But no Miss Lee. We even went as far away as a small stone building with iron bars on the windows. The entrance was covered with crude wooden planks and had a huge ancient bolt that was too stiff to move. I climbed on to Shane's shoulders to peer through the bars on the high window.

'What can you see?' Shane grunted.

'Nothing,' I said. 'Pitch black. But there's a strange smell.'

'Cow dung,' suggested Shane.

'No,' I sniffed again. 'A smell that's kinda like a mixture of rotten stuff and sort of sweet lemons.'

'How can you tell the difference?' Shane laughed as he dumped me from his shoulders. 'Did the lemon smell go into one nostril and the rotten smell go up the other nostril? Nice one, Milo. You could join a circus as the Great Smelly Master. People would be invited to hold stuff under your nose and you'd identify the smells. And I'd be your assistant, of course ...'

'You're mad,' I said.

'Yeah, well speaking of mad, we'd best get back,' Shane said. 'Gran will hold back my ice-cream dessert if I'm late. What will you do with the shoes?'

'I'll bring them with me,' I said, not really thinking ahead.

'Bring where?' Shane asked.

'I don't know yet,' I replied.

'You should give those shoes to your dad,' Shane said. 'That's evidence, that is.'

'Maybe,' I sighed. 'But if I show them to him he'll want to know where I found them.'

'So?' Shane shrugged his shoulders.

'Well, I've come much farther than the two-mile distance I'm allowed on my bike, so I'd be in worse trouble. I'll think of something. Unless,' I went on, 'unless maybe you'd hide them?'

'No way,' said Shane, holding up his two hands.

However, the matter was taken out of our hands when we saw two familiar figures walking towards us.

'Oh no,' said Shane. 'Look who's here.'

'Ha, if it isn't our two friends Porky and Worm,' laughed Wedge. 'What are you guys doing on our patch?'

'It isn't your patch,' Shane said, with a poor attempt at a snarl.

'I hope you two haven't nicked the tin that we sell for good money,' said Crunch. 'See, me and Wedge here have a nice little number in selling old tin things for melting down.'

'Yeah, and we don't want anyone butting in on our turf,' added Wedge. 'This place,' he went on, waving around the whole wasteland, 'is ours – mine and Crunch's.'

'Well. You can have it,' I said, trying to keep cool.

'Especially that smelly stone house,' put in Shane, pointing to it. 'Just your sort of mucky place.'

I closed my eyes and waited for the battle to begin. Nothing happened.

Wedge and Crunch were looking at one another with dismay.

'You went there?' said Crunch, his face actually scared.

Wedge grabbed my jacket and pulled me closer to his mean face. 'What did you see?' he snarled.

'N-nothing,' I tried to snarl back. 'It's just a smelly—'

That's when one of Miss Lee's red shoes fell from my jacket.

Wedge and Crunch stared at the red shoe.

'That's Miss—' began Crunch before

Wedge stamped on his toe.

'Shut up,' he snarled.

For a big chap, Shane can make a good move when he wants to. Quick as a flash, he scooped up the shoe and pedalled away, with me after him.

'Hey! You get back here!' Wedge yelled. 'We're not finished.'

'As if!' Shane yelled back.

We rode away like bats in a gale.

When we got to my house, I took the shoe from Shane, wrapped it with the other one in my jacket and put them on the carrier.

'Aren't you going to show them to your dad?' Shane asked.

'Later on maybe,' I said.

'So,' he went on. 'Where are you going tonight? Are your mum and dad going too? And why's it a problem?'

'Oh, stop asking me questions!' I groaned,

and then felt awful for talking to my best friend like that. 'Sorry, Shane,' I went on. 'It's just something I have to do on my own.'

'Yeah, right,' Shane muttered. 'Well I hope you'll enjoy – whatever.'

I bit my lip while I watched him cycle away, and I so wished I could tell him what I had to do. I'd never felt so alone in all my life. And scared. Very scared. Too scared.

'Wait!' I shouted, running after him. 'I'll tell you ...'

But he didn't hear me.

I stashed Miss Lee's shoes away in my bike carrier and trudged into the house like a condemned man.

CHAPTER NINE

THE SEARCH CONTINUES

'Not hungry, Milo?' Mum asked at dinner. 'I made your favourite, shepherd's pie with grated cheese. Have you been munching chocolate with Shane?'

'No, Mum,' I said, pushing my fork around the plate. 'I'm just not really hungry.'

Luckily, Dad arrived before Mum could ask more questions.

'Sorry I'm late,' he said. 'Bit of a crisis,' he went on as he hung his coat on a chair. 'Miss Lee is missing. We've been searching everywhere. Her car is outside her house. The driver's door was open, and her school stuff was scattered along the footpath.'

'Oh, that's awful,' said Mum. 'She must have forgotten to lock it.'

'I don't think so,' Dad went on. 'It's more than that. We've brought in extra gardaí to help the search. I'm going back later.'

'Have you searched that stony place where the old cottages are, Dad?' I asked. I didn't want to let on where I'd been, but I was trying to give Dad a hint.

'Good idea, son,' said Dad. 'I'll get on to that before the sun goes down. Though I can't think what Miss Lee would be doing out in that desolate, stony place. Pass the ketchup, lad.'

'Why is it so stony, Dad?'

'Oh, those stones have been there for hundreds of years,' said Dad. 'First of all there was a castle there.'

'Really?' I exclaimed.

'Yes. Oh, way back around the thirteen or fourteen hundreds. The town castle survived, but the other one fell into ruins. Perhaps its owners left because it was so far from the shops,' he said, grinning.

'Two castles just a few miles away from each other?' I said. 'That's strange.'

'Nothing was strange in those days,' said Dad. 'Anywhere you go in Ireland you'll see ruined castles. The country is littered with them. If we knocked them down and used the stones, we could join up with the Great Wall of China.'

Sometimes I think my dad's sense of humour is plugged into a different planet. But I made a decision. Shane was right – I needed to show Dad those shoes. When Dad and I had cleared the table, I waited until Mum went out to bring in clothes from the line, then I dashed down the hall to get the shoes. I shouldn't have stopped for a wee, because by the time I'd washed my hands, I heard Dad call out to Mum and then the car starting up. I struggled out of the downstairs loo and ran down the hall, but the car was already gone. I felt a right idiot. I should have been upfront and told Dad everything. I thought about phoning him, but I was sure he'd be mad I hadn't told him.

Later on, when I headed off to bed at nine o'clock, I lay there with my clothes on and waited for the town clock to chime ten thirty.

Worrying about Miss Lee and, worst of all, being scared of having to honour what Mister Lewis thought was my promise of help, I just wished I could pull the bedclothes over my head and not wake up until morning. But that wasn't going to happen. I couldn't let my old spooky friend down. I waited until I heard Mum snoring and slipped out through the living-room window.

CHAPTER TEN

SHANE MAKES A NEW FRIEND

At the bottom of Main Street my belly turned to jelly when the castle loomed eerily against the moon. There was nobody around the dim back entrance. I'd kind of hoped there might be lots of people walking past, or chatting at the gate and I'd have to go home. Or maybe the gate would be fixed and I couldn't get in. But that would have stamped me as a cowardly geek for the rest of my life.

I wheeled my bike through the narrow opening. The ordinary sounds of the town were cut off. The big courtyard was silent and the moon shadows scary.

'Ah, Milo my boy,' the comforting sound of Mister Lewis's voice echoed across the courtyard. 'We're on the steps at the castle door,' he went on.

Then two things happened. As Mister Lewis stood up, a gust of wind whipped his lopsided hat from his head.

'Ah, me hat!' he cried out.

'Hey, Milo!' another voice called out from behind me. It was Shane, wheeling his bike!

I was really glad to see him.

'Look what blew into me,' he shouted, waving Mister Lewis's hat. 'The Cat in The Hat,' he said, laughing.

'You followed me, Shane!' I said.

'Of course,' he said. 'You didn't think I'd let you off on your own, did you? I knew you were scared about having to do something you didn't want to do, so I watched from my window and followed. And here I am. What's up?'

'Thank you for retrieving my hat, young man,' said Mister Lewis, wafting over.

'Wow! How did you do that, Mister?'

'Do what, boy?' said Mister Lewis.

'Your feet hardly touched the ground,' said Shane.

'I always walk like this,' Mister Lewis replied sniffily.

'Cool,' said Shane. 'Are you part of a circus?'

'Shane!' I put in. 'This is *Mister Lewis*.'

'Hi, Mister,' said Shane. 'So,' he went on, turning to me. 'What's the crack? What are we doing here?'

'Mister Lewis,' I said again, slowly, nodding towards my very old friend.

'I know. I heard you the first time.' Then he turned to Mister Lewis. 'The man who lived in the house where we live was called Mister Lewis too,' said Shane.

'Ah, that would be me,' Mister Lewis said, putting his hat on.

'No,' said Shane. 'That Mister Lewis died years and years ago.'

'I did indeed,' said Mister Lewis, smiling.

That's when Shane slid in a heap to the ground.

CHAPTER ELEVEN

THE PORTAL

'Is this some sort of nightmare, Milo?' Shane gasped, still sitting on the ground. 'Tell me it is and that I'll wake up in a minute.'

'No nightmare, my boy,' said Mister Lewis. 'You caught me off my guard. Just think of me as a harmless old spook with a mission. Milo has come to help.'

'That's what I wanted to ask you, Mister Lewis,' I put in. 'What do you want me to do?'

'All in good time, Milo. All in good time. Besides,' he added, 'you have your friend now to help you.'

Well, that was no comfort at all – Shane can be a bit of a blunderer.

'Now, let us all go inside,' said Mister Lewis, pointing to the steps leading up to the big door of the castle.

'Hey, Milo, we get to go inside and see all the work that's been done? Cool,' said Shane as he heaved himself up and brushed the dust off his behind.

'Don't you want to go home, Shane?' I whispered. 'Didn't you hear? Mister Lewis is a ghost.'

'Aw, that's alright, Milo,' he said. 'If you're OK with that, then I'm OK too.'

'Park your bicycles, boys, and come along,' Mister Lewis called out as he headed up the steps. Beyond the big outer door there was an even bigger one that looked much older than the first door. There were weird carvings on it and stained glass with strange lettering.

Before putting his hand on the big handle with brass snakes on it, Mister Lewis turned and looked at us, talking in a ghostly-rattling breath.

'Are you sure you want to come through?' he asked, hesitating for a moment.

'Of course we do,' said Shane. 'We've been dying to see inside, haven't we, Milo?'

Not late at night. I thought. I didn't say that, of course. I'd never live it down if I chickened out.

When we followed Mister Lewis through that inner door, both Shane and I gasped as a sort of warm breeze wrapped itself around us and there was a low sound that's hard to describe. Think about the sound of a radio when you fiddle with the controls – like, strange, muffled voices and bits of music all mixed up together. But once we were through the door, all that simply stopped.

'Where's the music and the people?' asked Shane.

Mister Lewis shrugged his skinny shoulders. 'I didn't hear anything unusual.'

I looked to see if his ears were intact. They were. Maybe he was just used to strange sounds, being a ghost and all. Anyway, the sounds were gone. I figured some watchman had turned off the radio to have a nap.

The lights were on in the huge hall – not electric ones, just candles that sputtered in the breeze from the closing door. I thought it strange to have lights on at this hour, until I remembered that the great opening was in two days' time, so they must be working late to make sure everything was totally finished.

71

'Where is everyone?' I asked.

'Asleep, I'd say,' replied Mister Lewis.

'They sleep here?' I said. 'So, no rushing to get here on time in the morning. Cool thinking.'

'Well, actually, Milo,' began Mister Lewis. 'There's something I need to—'

'Oh, wow!' Shane interrupted, looking around the big hall. 'This is awesome. And look at the heads stuck on the wall, Milo! Deer with huge antlers – you'd never get one of those animals into a horsebox!'

There were huge curtains hanging along the high walls, with stitched pictures on them of knights in armour, and fat women bursting out of long dresses.

'Ah, you're admiring the fine tapestries, Milo,' said Mister Lewis. 'I knew you were a cultured chap.'

'Cultured? You?' Shane sniggered in my

ear as we followed Mister Lewis into a big room. Sitting at a long table, his chin resting on his hands was Ossie, still looking grim and grumpy.

'What are *they* doing here?' he muttered. 'Why have you brought them through the portal? They are strange and have bad clothing and peculiar hats.'

'Hey, excuse me, Miss Fancy Pants,' snorted Shane. 'I paid a fortune for this jacket with my own money. It's almost real leather. And these aren't hats, they're cycle helmets.'

I groaned. This was all I needed – NOT!

'Hush, Shane,' I whispered. 'He's a boy.'

Shane looked at me, his eyes out on stalks.

'You're kidding me,' he said with a laugh.

I shook my head.

'What kind of a place is this, Milo?' Shane whispered. 'It's the middle of the night and we're in the castle with a man wearing the

Cat's Hat and a skinny guy who wears girl's clothes. Please tell me I'm dreaming.'

'No dream, boy,' chuckled Mister Lewis. 'No dream at all. We just have to go on, eh, an important mission, as it were.'

'Cool,' Shane said, thumping my arm. 'If you're up for it, Milo, then so am I.'

I sighed. No turning back now.

'Wonderful. Come with me, boys, to the battlements,' said Mister Lewis in a low voice. 'And that means you too, Ossie.'

'Osgur,' the boy growled. 'And I'm not going up there. It's too cold.'

'Yeah, yeah. Whatever,' retorted Mister Lewis, winking at me, because I'd taught him some proper modern expressions on his last visit. Before we followed Mister Lewis up a winding stone stairs where fiery torches in iron brackets were lighting the way, he turned and put his finger to his lips.

'Stay very quiet, boys,' he whispered.

'Why?' asked Shane.

'The night watch,' Mister Lewis said softly.

Well, that was fair enough, I thought. It must be the most boring job. No wonder a watchman needs a radio and a nap. Now and then, we stopped to look out through the slotted openings.

'This is awesome, Milo,' whispered Shane, folding his arms against the cold breeze that blew in. 'But why didn't they put glass in those skinny little windows when they were doing up the castle?'

'Those narrow slits are for the archers to shoot their arrows,' said Mister Lewis.

'Archers? Wow,' said Shane. 'This gets better and better, Milo.'

I have to say I didn't share his enthusiasm. Where were we going, and what were we supposed to do?

CHAPTER TWELVE

MISTER LEWIS EXPLAINS

My leg muscles were screaming by the time we got to the top of the winding steps. Mister Lewis got me and Shane to push open a big door on to the battlements. It's his hands, you see. Being a ghost, he can't do much pushing because they would just go through the wood.

'We're here. Sshh,' he whispered, putting

his fingers to his lips again. 'Just wait here a moment,' he went on. 'I'll have a look around to see if the coast is clear before you come out.'

'Ha, you're going to go invisible,' I giggled. 'You don't want to scare the watchman.'

'Eh, something like that,' he said before disappearing.

'How did he do that, Milo?' whispered Shane.

'Because he's a ghost, Shane.'

'A real ghost! Are you serious? So you weren't joking me!'

'That's right,' I said.

'Hm, fair enough,' whispered Shane.

See what I mean? Nothing panics Shane – except maybe when he first meets a dead man.

Mister Lewis wafted back after a minute or two, the moonlight shining through one of the skinny windows, showing up his puzzled frown.

'Strange,' he said, 'No watch outside. Battlements are empty.'

'He probably went down for a sandwich, or something,' I said.

Mister Lewis shook his head. Just a slight shake in case he'd lose some bits, as happens when he gets excited.

Well, there wasn't much to see when we went on to the battlements.

'They've turned off all the lights in town!' exclaimed Shane. 'Look. Milo. Look at how dark it is. The houses and streets have no lights.'

'Electricity wires must be down,' I said.

'Well,' said Mister Lewis, 'it's just the old part of the town in the area around the castle which is in darkness.'

'That's weird,' I said. 'You'd think if one part

goes then the whole lot would go too. That has happened during bad thunderstorms ...'

'Well,' put in Mister Lewis again, 'we're sort of in a different era just now.'

'How do you mean?' asked Shane.

'Listen carefully,' Mister Lewis said, pointing in the distance. 'You see where those trees are against the moonlight?'

'Yeah, that's where we live,' said Shane. 'Me and Milo live over there.'

'Right,' Mister Lewis went on. 'That's the newer part of town. The *now* part. And you see where we're standing here?'

'Yes, of course we know. We're on the *then* castle,' I quipped. 'Get it?'

The old guy's brain is going down the tubes, I thought. Should we leave, Shane and me, before we get caught up in a dead man's ramblings?

'We are indeed, Milo,' he said. 'But we're

not in the *now*.'

'What's he talking about, Milo?' whispered Shane.

I was too scared to ask.

Then Mister Lewis gave a slight cough before saying words I would never have expected to hear.

'We're, eh, back in the fourteen hundreds,' he said. 'But don't worry,' he went on, as Shane's chin slipped down to his chest and my knees buckled like boiled chicken legs. 'It's just for a little while – until I get Ossie sorted.'

I noticed he crossed his fingers as he said that. Did that mean we might be stuck here in the past for longer? Forever even? I wanted to faint and wake up in my bed. But, hey, Mister Lewis was my good, if deceased, buddy, and buddies don't mess with their pals.

Shane squeezed my arm, really hard. 'Hey Milo,' he whispered. 'I think I'd actually like to go now. Right now,' he added. 'We've seen enough. I don't much like this century.'

Before I could croak an answer, Mister Lewis herded us over to another vantage point on the battlements.

'You see that light?' he said, pointing away in the distance.

Sure enough, when we squinted our eyes we could see flickering lights far away through the trees.

That,' said Mister Lewis, 'is where we must go on your bicycles, across an ancient track. The town, the people and this castle are depending on you two chaps, and Ossie and me.'

Well, Shane and I looked at one another. I hoped he wasn't going to fall down in a faint again because I needed him as he was the only other live person here. Spooks are OK in their own way, but when the chips are down you want a warm-blooded mate to be with you.

CHAPTER THIRTEEN

THE GRANT

'Depend on us to do what?' I almost didn't want to know, but if you're several centuries away from home, you need to know these things.

'Well, just trust me, Milo,' said Mister Lewis.

Those were not the words I wanted to hear. Much as I like my spooky friend, there's always the danger that he'll disappear, and we'd be, like, shuffling about in an age that didn't have X-boxes or ice cream, forever.

'Now let's go back downstairs and sort things out,' said Mister Lewis, giving another glance around the dark battlements.

'Still no sign of the watchman?' I whispered.

He sighed and whispered a quiet 'no'.

Just as well, I thought. Being caught by any watchman is not funny. But facing a fourteenth-century one was more than nerves could stand.

'Why me and Shane, Mister Lewis?' I asked. 'We're just regular kids. What can we do?'

'Yeah,' added Shane. 'I was only following Milo. I'm not into this sort of stuff.'

'Ha! Well you are now, lad,' said Mister Lewis.

'So why us?' I went on.

'Your friendship, Milo,' Mister Lewis replied. 'Who else could I turn to in an emergency like this? And, of course, your trusty bicycle.'

'My bike?'

'Indeed, I remembered your bicycle from the last time we worked together. It is silent and fast. What better way to get from one castle to another? And,' he added, rubbing his spooky hands together, 'thanks to Shane joining us, we now have *two* bicycles to take us there.'

'You mean that castle that we saw from the tower?' I asked.

I was beginning to sense a black shadow drifting inside my head. You know those nightmares caused by a late supper of fish and chips, and chocolate that the minder gets in when your parents are out? Except that there was no nightmare here. It was the real thing.

'Why should we go there?' asked Shane.

'One visit to an ancient castle is enough.'

'All in good time, Shane,' sighed Mister Lewis. 'Let's go downstairs. Quietly,' he added. 'Mustn't waken the sleeping inhabitants.'

There was no sign of Ossie when we went down to the big hall.

'I hope that grumpy kid has gone to bed,' I whispered to Shane.

'Looks like he has,' said Shane. 'Good riddance.'

'Why the grin? Are you not scared?' I asked him. 'You and me, we're way back in a time when anything might happen, and you're grinning like a chimpanzee with a bucket of bananas.'

Shane just shrugged his shoulders. 'Well, I'm not really scared any more. I'm with *you* and I trust *him*,' he nodded towards Mister Lewis. 'So, what's to worry?'

That was fair enough, I figured. If he could stamp down panic, so could I.

As we stood around the dying fire in the big hall and thawed out our fingers, Mister Lewis explained some of the history – not that I'm a fan of history, but when you're actually in it, it needs your full attention.

'A man called Rory Rua – Rory the Red because of his red hair – built this castle in the fourteen hundreds,' Mister Lewis began. 'He was a good man, kind to his wolfhounds, his falcons, and his family – in that order,' he added. 'And he only allowed hangings and floggings on sunny days to make the culprits feel good.'

'Nice man. OK,' I said, pushing Mister Lewis to get to whatever we needed to know.

'A decent sort, as noblemen go,' went on Mister Lewis, ignoring my hopping from one foot to the other, 'but Rory's jealous, greedy cousin, Roc, wanted to oust Rory from this fine castle. He took over a smaller neighbouring castle – you saw the lights of it from the battlements – and was preparing his men for a battle. But when Rory heard of this he hid the Grant.'

'The what?'

'The Grant was a valuable document, signed by the King, giving a nobleman land and permission to build a castle,' he explained. 'When Rory heard that his enemy, Roc, was nearby, he hid that Grant. If Roc got his hands on it, Rory would lose everything. No banks back then,' he continued. 'So people had to protect their valuables—'

'Just like now,' Shane interrupted. 'That's why I keep my bike in my bedroom. And I chain it to my bed—'

'So what has this to do with us?' I interrupted.

'Well, this is the thing,' Mister Lewis sighed. 'An architect in your time, who was working in this castle, found a leather pouch under a stone slab on one of the upper windows. Inside it was a parchment ...'

'The Grant!' I exclaimed.

'The very Grant,' Mister Lewis nodded. 'Written in Latin.'

'And what did it say?' Shane interrupted again. 'How could he understand the funny swirly writing that was used back then? They wrote with feathers in those days, didn't they?'

'I'm coming to that,' said Mister Lewis. 'Heavens, boy, you do go on!'

'Can you make it short, Mister Lewis?' I whispered. 'Get to the point.'

'Well,' he began. 'He gave it to his nice

lady friend for safekeeping, an educated teacher lady who said she'd find out more about it.'

A cold feeling iced its way up my neck. 'Miss Lee,' I whispered.

'That's her,' said Mister Lewis. 'Nice lady. Smart sense of style, and great teeth. And, by the way, she's a descendant of the same Rory Rua.'

'Miss Lee?!' said Shane. 'Cool.'

'So that's why she was always hanging around the castle,' I exclaimed.

'She wasn't at school,' Shane put in. 'We had to suffer the super hairy principal. All day!'

'Her car was found,' I said. 'The doors were open, and there were papers strewn around. Do you think it was spooks looking for the Grant?'

'If they'd found it,' Shane said, 'they

wouldn't have needed to kidnap her. So she must be hiding with it somewhere.'

'There were extra gardaí brought in to look for Miss Lee,' I added.

'Mister Lewis shook his head carefully. 'Well, they won't find her,' he sighed. 'Nobody will.'

'Why not?' Shane asked.

I'd gone dumb.

'Because Roc found his way to your time and he has abducted her,' Mister Lewis went on. 'She's imprisoned somewhere in his castle. And it's up to us to find her and prevent Roc from getting that Grant.'

'Why?' I asked. 'Just for an ancient a piece of paper …?'

'Because,' Mister Lewis interrupted, in a low tone of voice, 'if he gets his hands on that Grant, then this town will never have existed, nor the people who live here.

So that's why I've brought you here, you
and your bikes and—' But before he could
continue, Ossie came barging in, red-faced
and angry.

CHAPTER FOURTEEN

OSSIE GOES BERSERK

'Where have you all been? I've been looking for you all over the place – even the dark west battlements – ALL ON MY OWN!' Ossie ranted, waving what looked like a small wooden club – as if that would have sent the enemy running!

'Calm down, Ossie,' said Mister Lewis. 'You're in a right state. We were on the south battlements. What is your problem?'

'Master Lewis!' Ossie erupted like a mini volcano, all red-faced and spewing little spitlets. 'They're all asleep in the kitchen.'

'Of course they're asleep, lad. That's why you asked me to come and help you at this time of night,' said Mister Lewis.

'Those soldiers, who are supposed to be on watch, looking out for Roc and his men at the outer castle walls,' Ossie panted. 'They've been drinking apple wine. Someone must have put a potion in their food and water, and the wine. They're all asleep. I couldn't waken them, not even when I thumped them with Mistress Kate's heavy pan. All the kitchen staff are sleeping on the floor. Even the hounds are snoring. And I couldn't waken my mother, father or sisters in their beds!'

'Aha, so that's why there was nobody on guard!' said Mister Lewis, getting up from his chair.

Ossie's white face went even whiter. 'What will we do now?' he said, spluttering with fury.

I hadn't known that dead guys have spit – but then I realised that he was back in his own time.

'Roc will come and there will be nobody to stop him from taking over our castle – especially now that he probably has the Grant.'

'Oh, chill up, boy,' said Mister Lewis. 'I thought this would be an easy job to slip into Roc's castle, get Miss Lee and the Grant and head back to the present.'

Mister Lewis fiddled with his hat as he thought.

We waited and waited for him to come

up with an idea. From the look on his face, it didn't look like anything was stirring in his mind.

After a few moments, Shane spoke. 'I'm starving,' he said, looking at Ossie. 'Is there any food?'

'Are you mad?' I cried. 'We're facing the rest of our lives trapped in a freezing castle and all you can think of is food! And anyway Ossie said the food was drugged!'

The three of us jumped when Mister Lewis leapt up, waving his hands and dancing about on his skinny legs.

'FOOD!' he shouted. 'That's it. FOOD!'

Now I knew that his time had come. The spook had finally flipped. He was stone mad. We were really going to be stuck here forever, me and Shane, wearing tights and ploughing through cold muck and horse-dung (I've seen the films).

'Food?' I cried out. 'Are you crazy too, Mister Lewis? This isn't a time for food!' Oh shoot! The old guy's dead brains had finally kicked in. I sat on a stool, put my head on my hands and groaned.

'Shane,' Mister Lewis said, 'Your gran, Big Ella, bless her, is a food-loving lady, isn't that so?'

'Yeah. Me too,' Shane replied. 'What's that got to do with anything?'

My head sank further into my hands.

'Her cupboards are filled with all sorts of strange ingredients,' Mister Lewis continued.

'How do you know that?' said Shane, frowning. 'Have you been poking about in our cupboards?

'Of course I have. And I've often marvelled at the jars of exotic ingredients she gets from her friends in Africa, and other parts of the world. What else is there to do for entertainment at nights when you're dead? Now, listen closely. Here's my plan, boys. Then get those bicycles. There's much work to be done.'

CHAPTER FIFTEEN

BIG ELLA'S PLAN

We whooshed out through the fancy inner door, which Mister Lewis explained was a portal that could take us from past to present, as well as from present to past. We weren't really listening, Shane and me – we were so relieved to be back in our own time.

'There are two kinds of portals,' Mister Lewis was going on. 'There's the castle one and the natural arboreal one ...'

But we'd lost interest because we were

trying to get Ossie on to the carrier of Shane's bike.

'It's a wicked thing,' he cried, putting his club into a belt round his middle. 'I won't touch it.'

It was only when Shane gave him half a sticky Crunchie that we got him aboard. Mister Lewis wafted along beside me.

Then a thought struck me. 'Hey, Mister Lewis,' I called out, 'what's going to be outside the castle gates? I'm a bit confused, like, I don't know what century to expect.'

'No worries, lad,' he shouted. 'Once we're beyond the castle everywhere will be as you know it.'

'Really? We're really back in our own time? Are you sure?'

'Trust me, Milo,' he added. 'All is the same out there as it was yesterday. Are you having second doubts, lad?' he whispered.

I glanced around at Ossie, his hands clutching Shane's back. He's rude, bossy and a proper little upstart, I thought. But the other side of my brain put in the thought that if it was me trying to save my family, I'd be just like him. So, before the surging longing of turning towards home took over, I shook my head. 'No,' I sighed. 'No second thoughts.'

'I knew you'd say that,' said Mister Lewis. 'Good man.'

Well, that was no help. I was still as scared as a trapped mouse in a cattery.

'Shane,' Mister Lewis called out behind us. 'Follow us to Big Ella's.

'No way!' shouted Shane. 'She'll eat me alive and spit out me bones for sneaking out this late.'

'Don't be crude, boy. Your granny and I have met before.'

I knew that, of course, because I'd been there when there was this incident with a druid. But that's another story. I'd never told Shane what had really happened. I was forbidden by Big Ella to tell him. Not ever.

The street was quiet as we pedalled towards Shane's house.

'I'm not sure I want to do this,' said Shane. 'Big Ella will have a gigantic hissy fit, and I'll be grounded for years until I have no teeth and am too old to ride my bike.'

The lights were on downstairs. That was no surprise, when Big Ella gets a notion to paint a picture she goes for it straight away. Shane stood behind me as Mister Lewis 'cooeed' through the letterbox that Ossie held open. The door was flung open and Big Ella stood there with a dripping paintbrush in her hand. Shane clutched my arm. Like, I was going to protect him? But her face beamed when Mister Lewis moved in front of her.

'Mister Lewis!' she exclaimed. 'How wonderful to see you again. Come in, come in,' she went on, standing aside. Then she saw Shane. We waited for her shrill yell, but she just shook her head and smiled. 'You two boys been with Mister Lewis? That's good. And who is this, um, pretty little girl?'

'I'M NOT A GIRL!' shrieked Ossie. 'I AM THE SON OF RORY RUA.'

'Whatever you say, honey. Come along in.'

Shane let out the breath he'd been holding, and it went right down the back of my neck. I glanced up the road to my house and was glad to see that the lights were out, which meant that Mum was asleep. Dad wouldn't be back from night duty until tomorrow morning. I hoped I would be there in the flesh to say 'Hi, Dad', and not wafting about as a ghost. I almost bit my lip totally off my face as I forced myself to go into Big Ella's house instead of racing home.

Big Ella shooed us all into her big kitchen that smelled of all kinds of spices, fruit and paint.

'Ah, my old kitchen,' said Mister Lewis, sitting into a chair. 'Everything, looks good, lady,' he sighed. 'I feel so at home.'

Which was quite true. He had lived here years and years ago before he made a bad mistake and was destined to mooch around the garden as a ghost for years and years. Until he met me of, course. And I saved him – sort of.

'You have turned it into a very cosy place,' he said to Big Ella.

'You come back here any time you want, Mister Lewis,' she said. 'Now, what can I do for you folks?'

Mister Lewis took a deep sniff. 'Am I dreaming, or is that cocoa I'm smelling?

'It is indeed, Mister Lewis,' chuckled Big Ella. 'I like a mug of hot cocoa when I'm painting late at night. Would you like some?'

Mister Lewis shook his head sadly. 'Oh, I would love a mug of cocoa,' he sighed. 'It's been so many years since I tasted cocoa, but it's the hands, you see, my good lady,' he went on, holding them up. 'No substance. The darned things just go through everything.'

'No worries,' said Big Ella, rummaging in a drawer and producing a pair of woolly gloves with spaceship patterns on them. 'Let's try these for size.'

'My good space gloves!' Shane spluttered.

'Good space gloves?' echoed Big Ella. 'You've never even worn them, boy. "Too babyish" you said. But I could knit some more,' she said as she put them on Mister

Lewis's hands.

'Aw, it's OK,' Shane muttered.

'Thank you, lad,' said Mister Lewis, holding up his woolly hands and reaching for a spoon on the table. We all held our breath. And then he did it – he picked up the spoon!

'Look!' he exclaimed, holding up the spoon. 'It stays in my hand.'

'That's just grand,' laughed Big Ella. 'Now perhaps you can have a mug of cocoa.'

Mister Lewis's face lit up like a beacon. So we all had mugs of cocoa to celebrate. And, wonder of wonders, Ossie's face turned positively angelic as he downed 'this strange and wonderful nectar' as he called it.

CHAPTER SIXTEEN

SMELLY POTIONS

Being a well-mannered gentleman, Mister Lewis told Big Ella all about why we needed to sort out Roc and his gang and save our castle and the town. At first, she looked at me and Shane and shook her head. I must admit that I kinda hoped she'd put a stop to us getting involved. But then, she simply nodded and said, 'Well, let's see what we can do, eh?'

'If you had something that might make

those thugs fall asleep,' began Mister Lewis.

'Oh, I have a much better idea,' Big Ella chuckled. 'Clear the table, folks. There's work to be done.'

Big Ella got us to carry boxes and small bottles from her 'witchy den' as Shane calls it. She put on a big apron and set to work, mixing foul-smelling powders, puke-yellow potions and slimy green stuff. Every now and then she held up a strange little bottle of gunge and explained its use.

'Golden Seal,' she said. 'From the root of American crowfoot family.'

'What does it do, Gran?' asked Shane.

Big Ella just tapped her nose. 'You'll find out,' she announced.

Other strangely named stuff such as arrowroot and horsetail. 'For the kidneys,' she added. 'And this,' she said, holding up a small plant. 'This is clary sage.'

'What's that for?' I asked.

'Explosions,' Big Ella laughed.

'Bombs?' exclaimed Shane. 'Cool.'

'Not quite,' Big Ella chuckled. 'But mixed with this other stuff it will ...'

'Cause thunderous gas,' Mister Lewis interrupted.

When everything was stirred and bottled, Big Ella put her hands on her hips and looked at the four of us.

'So, tell me,' she began. 'How do you folks hope to get inside Roc's castle?'

'Erm,' began Mister Lewis, taking off his hat and scratching his head with the gloves.

'You haven't thought it through, have you?' sighed Big Ella.

'I thought perhaps we could sneak into the kitchen,' Mister Lewis began.

'SNEAK?' barked Big Ella. 'You don't SNEAK, man. You go in with glory and splendour. Come on. Let's make you lot look majestic. Follow me.'

She led us upstairs to her bedroom.

'What's she going to do?' I whispered to Shane.

He shrugged his shoulders. 'How should I know? When Big Ella gets an idea, nothing will stop her.'

Big Ella flung open a big wardrobe and began taking out strange and dazzling clothes. She chose a mud-coloured cloak, put it over Ossie's shoulders and fastened it with a safety pin. 'There, lad,' she said. 'That will disguise your rich clothing.'

Mister Lewis asked Ossie if he'd ever met Roc.

'No. He's my father's enemy,' he said. 'He has never been to our castle, nor I to his.'

'Well, that's good,' said Big Ella. 'He won't know who you are. Still,' she went on, 'perhaps you should stay away from him in case he sees a resemblance to your father.'

'Good thinking, lady,' said Mister Lewis.

Then Big Ella turned towards Shane and me.

'Now, you boys,' she said, looking at us up and down. 'How will we disguise you?'

'Minstrels, I think,' put in Mister Lewis. 'Minstrels are always welcome in castles.'

'Good thinking, Mister Lewis,' she said. 'Perfect.'

'Mmm,' Mister Lewis mused. 'A boy and a girl, wouldn't you say?'

'Decidedly,' Big Ella clapped her hands.

'Well, that'll be easy,' I giggled, nodding towards Ossie's long hair.

'Oh no,' Mister Lewis said. 'You'll make a wonderful girl, Milo. Ossie is fine as he is — a very fourteenth-century boy. But we need a lady minstrel.'

'No WAY!' I cried out.

Well, despite all my shouting and pushing and kicking, I was decked out in a long blue dress, Miss Lee's red shoes that Big Ella fetched from my bike and stuffed with rolled-up socks to make them fit. And, worst of all, a girlie bonnet with two yellow plaits attached. Talk about cringe!

'If you ever tell anyone about this,' I hissed at Shane. 'I'll clobber you, understand?'

'With what?' he laughed. 'One of your pigtails?'

It was only when Mister Lewis mentioned finding Miss Lee that I calmed down.

'Minstrels need musical instruments,' sighed Mister Lewis, scratching his chin.

'Done!' said Shane, running into his bedroom and arriving back, waving the guitar he'd got for Christmas. He handed me a small, long drum. 'That's a real ancient African armpit drum made of goatskin,' he said proudly. 'You put it under your arm and bang it with your other hand.'

'Yecch,' I muttered. I didn't know which was the most disgusting, the dead goat or the armpit. 'If you've had this under your armpit, I'm not using it!'

'Yes you will,' said Big Ella. 'OK?

'Yeah,' I muttered. Big Ella has that effect on people.

'Now Mister Lewis,' said Big Ella, turning to where the spook was sitting in an armchair. 'What can we do for you? How about a nice turban ...?'

'Nice nothing, thank you, lady,' he put in. 'I have the great power of stealth. I can be invisible.'

'Shame,' said Big Ella. 'You would look elegant in a turban.'

Mister Lewis scowled at Shane and me when we sniggered. 'Time to go,' he muttered.

We went downstairs and tied the box containing the weird potions, guitar and drum on Shane's carrier because it's bigger than mine.

That meant that I had to take Ossie on my bike. One moan from him, I told myself, and he's dumped. However, since I was stuck with a wig and a girlie bonnet, I gave him my bicycle helmet.

'Cool,' he said. Well, at least he was learning proper English.

'Hold on!' said Big Ella, running after us, carrying a big floppy hat with a feather on it. 'That's for you, Shane. It'll do as a minstrel's hat,' she said as she put it into the spice box.

'Why do I have to wear a poncy thing like that?' he cried. 'No way!'

'Because you have to look like a minstrel, lad,' put in Mister Lewis.

'HA!' I laughed. 'We're quits now.'

'Take care,' Big Ella called after us. 'Be brave, be careful, and do whatever Mister Lewis says.'

We'd gone about half a mile when Mister Lewis stopped us at the woods near the castle. He asked us to focus our lamps on him and we watched as he went around touching the trees.

'What is he at?' began Shane.

I sure hoped his mind hadn't flipped. You never quite know what a dead person gets up to. I mean – touching trees, for goodness sake!

'Ah here we are,' he said eventually, putting his hand on a gnarled old tree. 'The arboreal portal!'

'The what?' Shane and I exclaimed.

'Didn't you listen to me?' he said. 'When I was telling you about the different portals. This one is nature's arboreal portal – trees,

115

boys, as distinct from the indoor castle portal. Indeed,' he added, 'there is a third portal somewhere, but I've forgotten where.'

'Can we please get going, sire,' said Ossie. 'Time is running out.'

Mister Lewis nodded and placed his two hands on the tree and muttered something. A cold breeze whooshed out and a dark hole appeared.

'Quickly now,' said Mister Lewis. 'Nature's portal lasts only a few seconds. Turn off your lamps before we go through. Nature doesn't like artificial light.'

'Will it open this way when we come back?' asked Shane, before making a move.

'Eh,' Mister Lewis hesitated. 'Trust me,' he answered.

Well, those words didn't give out good vibes.

CHAPTER SEVENTEEN

AN ANCIENT WEDGE AND CRUNCH

The eerie sound of the trees closing when we were through was like a sinking-ship sort of feeling. Not that I'd ever been on a sinking ship, but I'm sure it gives out the same sort of panicky, whooshing sound.

Beyond the trees we came to a rough

117

track. I knew then that we really were back in the fourteen hundreds. We turned on our bicycle lamps even though the sky wasn't completely dark because of the full moon. Mister Lewis went ahead on the track to warn us of any holes or stones.

'Is it much farther?' moaned Shane. 'My bum is numb.'

'Never mind that. Just remember that you two boys are minstrels,' put in Mister Lewis. 'Do you have songs that you can sing?'

Shane and I glanced at one another. 'Of course we have,' said Shane. 'Loads of songs. No worries.'

No worries? At school Shane and I sang so badly that Miss Lee said we sounded like two over-excited geese. She insisted that we mime the songs whenever a school inspector or some posh bores came to visit. And now we were to sing to hairy soldiers who were about to go to battle!

So we tried a few bars of modern songs that scared night creatures into the trees

'Whoa!' yelled Ossie as he fell off my carrier and rolled himself into a ball on the ground screaming with laughter. 'If that's the sound of singing in your time, Shane, and if girls look like you, Milo, then I truly want to stay in this century!'

'We weren't that bad,' Shane muttered stroppily.

'Yes you were,' laughed Ossie, brushing his tunic and hopping back onto my carrier.

'I've heard worse,' said Mister Lewis, taking his mittened hands from his ears. 'However, I think the cocoa has gone to my head. It's been so many years since I've had a rich beverage. I need to rest a while. Don't worry. I'll catch up with you chaps shortly.'

Worry? Of course I worried. He was the only weapon we had on this creepy road hundreds of years from home. Anything could happen.

Sure enough, after about a mile, our lamps picked up two guys with bony legs ahead of us.

'Let's go,' Shane said, getting up speed and forging ahead.

The two men turned around. At first they looked scared, but when they saw we were kids, they stood out and put up their hands.

I almost fell of my bike when our lamps shone on two thin faces that had the mean looks of Wedge and Crunch!

'Yo, who goes there?' said the thinner one with a sneer. 'Are you young people out alone on this desolate pathway?'

'What wonderful contraptions are these?' interrupted the other one, standing right in front of Shane's bike.

'I think WE should be the ones to have such riches from these exotic foreigners,' said the Wedge-faced one. He put his ugly warty face up to mine. 'What do you think, my pretty damsel?' he asked, laughing, and went to join his mate who was pulling Shane off his bike. Whew, I have to admit that for one short, cowardly moment I was glad I was a girl.

I looked around, desperately wishing to hear Mister Lewis shout and float along to scare them.

'This is going to be nasty,' I muttered, getting ready to put down my bike and look for a stick. 'If they take that box of stuff from Shane's bike, we're totally doomed.'

That's when Ossie jumped off the back of my bike.

'Hey, Ossie, come back here,' I hissed. But

he took no notice. He put his hand to his belt and pulled out the mini club. Then he strode up to where the thugs were hassling Shane and tapped the taller one. I shut my eyes and waited for his scream. But it wasn't Ossie who screamed, it was the tall guy when Ossie kicked his knee with an expert blow that was way better than anything we'd learnt at *taekwan-do* class. As he went down, Ossie decked him on the nose with his club. When the other thug tried to grab Ossie, the kid stood his ground, lifted his leg and punched him in the belly with his dainty little foot, knocking him down like a sack of rubbish.

'Would you gentlemen like some more?' He laughed, waving his club.

'Ha!' he said proudly. 'My renowned Weapons Master has taught me the many ways of besting slime such as you.' Then he gave a loud 'YAAAGGGHHH!' and waved his club as he lunged at them again.

By the time Shane and I had scraped up the courage to help Ossie, the golden oldie bullies had upped and run across the dark, boggy land.

'Now,' said Ossie as calmly as if he had just chased away a fly. 'Let us go and do what we have to do.'

'Hey,' said Shane as Ossie jumped up on my bike. 'That was awesome the way you scared those morons!'

'Double awesome,' I added. 'You were red hot, Ossie.'

'What do those strange words mean?' Ossie asked. 'Do you mock me?' he added guardedly, his hand on his club.

'No way!' I exclaimed. 'It means total respect, man. You sent those guys running while we just stood scared.'

'Speak for yourself. Milo,' grunted Shane. 'I was just about to clobber them ...'

'With the feather from your fancy hat?' I said, and the three of us laughed loudly as we headed along the bumpy road.

CHAPTER EIGHTEEN

CYCLING THROUGH TIME

We could see the flickering lights of Roc's castle when Mister Lewis caught up with us.

'Sorry, boys,' he said as he wafted along beside us. 'I fell asleep under a tree. Imagine – the first sleep I've had for a hundred and two years. Thanks to your granny's cocoa, Shane. Luckily, I see your route along this road has been easy, so you didn't need my help.'

'No, good sire,' said Ossie. 'We simply swatted some buzzing flies.'

Mister Lewis tut-tutted when the three of us laughed loudly again.

However, we sobered up when we got close to the enormous gates of the castle.

'Remember not to reveal your name, Ossie,' whispered Mister Lewis. 'Roc is your father's enemy. We'll have to hide you from him, and give you a false name for the rest of the occupants of the castle.'

'Something modern,' suggested Shane. 'Something computerish.'

'Google,' I suggested. I don't know why; it just seemed to fit.

'Earth,' added Shane.

'Google Earth!' we said together.

'From Afar,' I added.

'Master Google Earth from Afar, Hmm,' mused Mister Lewis. 'I've never heard of it, but I like it.'

The two sentries who stood under flaming torches pointed their lances at us as we approached.

'Who goes there?'

'US!' Shane called out.

I groaned quietly. If he started messing about with these ancients, we could find ourselves in a black dungeon, rattling our chains, fighting with rats for mouldy crusts of bread, and having cockroaches crawling up our noses at night. My dad had told me how he often wished those punishments could come back into use on thugs in the twenty-first century. Dad, I sighed. Would I ever see him and Mum again?

I jumped when the gloves with the spaceship patterns landed on my shoulders.

'Listen to me and repeat what I say,' whispered Mister Lewis. 'And remember you're a girl, so act like one.'

His whispery voice was muffled by the plaits so it was hard to hear him.

'WE ARE MATCHSTICK DICTION-ARIES FROM AFAR,' I said in a high, girlie voice as I flicked my plaits.

'*DIGNITARIES!*' hissed Mister Lewis. '*MYSTIC DIGNITARIES!*'

But it didn't matter. These thugs didn't seem to know the difference.

'And I am Master Google Earth, the son of my Lord Google from Afar,' Ossie shouted, coming from behind and standing straight in front of the guards in his rich, red clothes, his shabby cloak flung behind him, his hands on his hips, like a regular little prince. 'I represent my eminent father who has sent us here. I bring his good wishes and two entertainers to amuse Lord Roc.'

Entertainers? Did he mean me and Shane? We couldn't entertain a cat with a toy mouse on a string, never mind a gang of loud soldiers.

Luckily, the guards were more interested in his blue cycle helmet than his words. But it was Shane who fascinated them the most. They had obviously never seen an African person before. They moved closer to him and put out their hands to touch his face. I hoped he wouldn't throw a hissy fit and bang their heads together. But he puffed out his chest and leaned towards them with a big toothy grin. 'I have come from the far-out land of magical YouTube, a country rich with Big Mac Burgers, donuts and moving pictures,' he boomed. (All his favourite things, of course). 'Want to see my tricks?'

What tricks? Shane was useless at tricks, even the ones in cheap Christmas crackers. With a great flourish, he rang the bell of his bicycle as hard as he could. Too hard, I thought. But it worked. The guards leapt back, their spears pointing at the bike.

'That is indeed a magical thing,' said the skinnier guard. 'More!' he ordered. 'Show us more.'

With another exaggerated flourish and even wider grin, Shane pressed the bell. No sound. He tried again and again, but there wasn't so much as a tweet. It had croaked. The guards muttered to one another, their faces grim. They raised their spears. Ossie pulled my arm. 'Come,' he said. 'We must help.'

I looked around frantically. Where was Mister Lewis when you needed him? Had the cocoa kicked in again and made him fall back asleep?

I should have known better. When I saw the spaceship gloves fly towards the thugs, I knew my spooky pal was up to his eerie tricks. He moved his gloves all around the guards, muttering any old words that came to mind: 'hoolah moola, loco cocoa, bikes and spikes, dead men coming, *waaaagh*!'

The guards clung to each other. But it was when the gloves touched their faces that they scarpered down the track, away from the castle.

'I shall be here waiting here for yooouuu!' We heard Mister Lewis call out in a ghostly voice as he drifted after them.

'A class act, Mister Lewis,' I said when he returned with his full body.

'Indeed,' he grinned, lovingly patting the gloves. 'But now to more serious matters.'

The dark courtyard was empty as we made

our way towards the castle, but we could hear sounds of laughter and rough shouting through the upstairs' windows

'Now, boys,' said Mister Lewis when we reached the steps of the castle. 'This is where we part company.' He lifted the box from Shane's bike. 'Ossie and I will find our way down to the kitchen and—'

'The kitchen?' interrupted Ossie. 'I don't frequent kitchens. They are used only by servants.'

'Well, you'd better get familiar with this one,' said Mister Lewis. 'You've dumped your disguise, so we'll all be in trouble if Roc recognises you in your princely clothes. Now, we must introduce ourselves to the kitchen staff as servants of the – eh – visiting guests upstairs.'

'What visiting guests?' I asked.

'You and Shane,' he replied. 'I shall tell

the kitchen staff that you've brought exotic spices from afar for us to prepare for Roc and his men. You two must present yourselves to Roc. Remember, you are entertainers.'

'What?' I said. 'You're leaving us alone!'

'Just keep Roc and his men occupied,' Mister Lewis went on, handing us the guitar and drum. 'They'll be "gobsmacked", as you say, Milo. Go now. There's much to do. Sing well.'

Sing? Me and Shane! We were dead already.

Upstairs, the shouting and laughing was even louder, just like the early afternoon slot in the cinema during the boring kissy parts of a film.

Shane looked at me as we hauled our bikes upstairs. 'Let me do the talking first,' he whispered, going ahead of me up the stairs. 'I think I have the right idea.'

133

'Huh?' I choked. The words 'right' and 'idea' weren't words you'd associate with Shane at a time like this.

The noise was deafening when we got to the top of the stairs and entered a huge room where soldiers were drinking from fat tankards. Everyone stopped as we went through. We made our way towards the far end of the room where a small group of men, dressed in posh clothes, sat around a table on a raised platform. The silence was pure scary. Then the shouting began again: soldiers pointing at us and our bikes and yelling.

On the platform, the man in the richest-looking clothes stood up from his chair. 'SILENCE!' he boomed, banging on the table. For a skinny guy with bad hair and a squashed nose he certainly knew how to get attention. The room hushed. 'To what do we owe this visit?' he went on when we'd leaned our bikes against the wall. 'Who has sent you strange people and your peculiar contraptions to my castle? And,' he added, leaning towards us, looking from one to the other in a puzzled sort of way. 'Why have you different skin?'

Darn! We hadn't thought of that. This needed a quick response.

Shane got there first. 'Girls are not allowed out in the sun,' he replied. 'We're like a draughts board when the family all get together,' he went on.

This really wasn't the time for bad jokes.

Nobody laughed. The total silence was weird.

I could almost hear Shane's brain clanking as he made up what to say next. As for me – my brain had shut down.

'We have been sent from Afar,' Shane

began. 'Our father is King Tayto, Lord of the Seas of North Africa. He has sent me, Sir Hamburger and my sister, the Lady Magenta Knickers, across the sea, to amuse and honour your worship, and bring friendship to him,' Shane went on, sweeping his feathered hat off his head and bowing low.

Magenta Knickers, indeed! He'd pay for that.

'Ho!' said Roc, who was obviously used to weird names. 'So my fame has spread to distant lands?'

'Yeah it has, sire,' Shane went on. 'King Tayto has heard about your conkers from his fleet of pirates ...'

'Conquests!' I hissed

'Pirates?' Roc was suddenly interested. 'Your father is a pirate king?' he said with awe.

'Indeed he is, sire,' replied Shane. 'The best.'

'Ah, I should like to meet your father,' said Roc.

'And he would like to join with you and your warriors, which is why he sent us to make our family known to you,' Shane went on, though he'd never even met his real father, who'd gone away after Shane's mother ran off with a wealthy rapper. Then Shane's granny brought him to Ireland when he was little.

'So, you have come to entertain?' went on Roc, settling back on his throne. 'Show us what you can do to please us? Tomorrow we go to battle.'

That got the rest of the men going. They banged their tankards on the long tables and yelled for action.

Shane looked at me, his eyes out on stalks.

'What'll we do now, Milo?'

'You're the one with the ideas,' I hissed. But this was no time for squabbling. 'We'd better sing.'

CHAPTER NINETEEN

RAPPERS

'We'll rap,' Shane whispered, settling the guitar strap over his shoulder. 'You don't need to sing for rap.'

'Rap? I don't know how to rap,' I began.

'I do,' Shane whispered. 'My mum sends CDs of rap to Gran. She listens to them all the time when she paints. Just say YO lots of times. And the words don't have to make sense. Just go with the flow.'

Great. Our lives depended on the word 'YO'!

'Right,' whispered Shane, strumming the guitar. 'You beat that drum. Here goes.' He cleared his throat and began.

YO, you guys, youse big and loud,
I'm thinkin' 'bout a big fat cloud
Yeah, yeah, rainy day
Lost my wellies in the hay
Let me tell ya 'bout mah dream
Of loadsa chips and choc ice cream.

Yep, that was typical of Shane. In spite of our serious predicament, his thoughts were on food. At first there was silence, and I could almost smell the dungeon already. But Roc stood up and clapped. Then the whole room exploded with clapping and shouting.

'More! More!' the soldiers were shouting and banging the tables.

Shane paused and strummed the guitar – totally out of tune.

'Your turn, Milo,' he whispered. 'While I make up another rap.'

Me? I tried to swallow, but I'd run out of spit.

'Just use your head,' murmured Shane.

'*Or listen man, we'll both be dead*,' he added softly as he strummed.

Well that kicked me into wake-up time. I beat the armpit drum and searched my mind for a starting word. I glanced at Shane, my best friend, trying to keep us both from a grim fate. We depended on each other, so I took a big breath and got going.

YO! I got an armpit drum
I'm a gal and I ain't dumb
YO! I'm rappin' really well
You guys' hair could do with gel

YO! YO! Sticky gel

Smelly, poncy, sticky gel. YO!

More clapping and shouting. Wow! Was this for real? Then Shane butted in with another finger-snapping rap:

I wanna be a real cool dude

Be mean and lean and deadly rude

Jus' like you guys 'n' Lord Roc

Who looks real groovy in his frock

YO! YO! He's the man

He's the man who's gonna eat

And sit all night on a pooey seat.

YO! YO! Hear the beat,

And slap the floor with ya' stinky feet!

YO!

The soldiers went wild. They got up, dancing to the beat and shouting for more.

Shane's face had the biggest grin I'd ever seen. We were the main cool dudes – real rap stars!

After a while, we were beginning to run dangerously out of wind and words.

'We can't go on much longer,' I panted in Shane's ear.

'I know,' he panted back. 'We'll have to do something else.'

'What can we do?' I went on. 'My throat is like broken glass and Miss Lee's shoes are killing me.'

'Our bikes!' Shane replied, still strumming his guitar. 'I bet they've never seen bikes in action, Milo.'

Then he turned to Roc and bowed again.

'And now, sire,' he said, 'me and my sister, Lady Magenta Knickers would like to demonstrate our ...' he paused and looked at me in desperation.

'Our amazing magical wheels,' I said, with quick thinking. 'Invented by a man of genius, whose wealth is so huge he has twelve strong men to stand guard over him in case thieves try to steal his plans.'

'Show me,' said Roc, standing up. 'Let me see how these strange things work.'

So we mounted our bikes and rode up and down the huge room. Then we got a bit braver and aimed at the soldiers' feet, avoiding them skilfully at the last second. How they screeched and laughed. And then we got really brave and did a few wheelies. The soldiers whooped and shouted at our skills.

Shane turned and winked at me. Big mistake. He accidentally rammed into a tough soldier with a face like a bad-tempered bull. The soldier jumped up and grabbed Shane's bike. 'Step back, boy,' he growled, pushing Shane away as if he was swatting a fly. 'I shall master this apparatus.'

Then my bike was pulled away by another thug. All we could do was stand and watch as they all fought over our bikes. Roc just sat on his throne, drinking more wine and laughing at the chaos. He probably thought this was part of the act. This wasn't meant to happen. If that lot got too pushy and knocked my pigtails off, I'd be exposed as a boy. Imagine trying to explain that! Up and down the Great Hall the soldiers took turns, veering into tables and knocking one another down. Shane and I tried to reach Roc and tell him this wasn't a good way to treat important visitors from Afar, but he was chatting with his captains.

Just as we felt everything was falling apart, servants arrived, with steaming platters, through a door behind Roc's throne. Our bikes were thrown down and the soldiers made a beeline for the tables.

'Come, sit with us, you children of King Tayto of Africa,' Roc called out to Shane and me.

Whew! This could be awkward. 'Listen,' I whispered in Shane's ear as we went towards the table, 'No matter how hungry you are, don't eat the food. We'll just kinda drop it on the floor. Got that?'

'Gotcha,' he hissed.

We watched as the soldiers grabbed the plates from the servants and dug into the meat and veg like snarling wolves.

The noise of soldiers slurping and guzzling echoed around the room, and the sweaty servants were running back and forth with second and third helpings.

'They haven't brought food here to Roc's table,' whispered Shane.

'I know,' I whispered back. At first I thought that this was some sort of strange ritual, but surely the Lord and his captains should be served first. I could see Shane's eyebrows go up higher and higher whenever the servants passed our table.

'Excuse me, Sir Roc,' he finally piped up. 'Have your servants forgotten this table?'

All the posh guys around the table laughed.

'Oh no, my boy,' said Roc. 'We would not partake of such slop. This food is only for the common soldiers. I and my captains – and you two guests, will dine on wild boar, salted fish, boiled fowl and eels in my private quarters.'

Shane and I looked at one another. If Roc and his snooty captains didn't eat Big Ella's concoction, we were absolutely doomed!

CHAPTER TWENTY

TRAPPED!

I leapt when I felt a tap on my shoulder. It was one of Mister Lewis's spaceship gloves. 'Well done, Milo,' he whispered in my ear. 'All is in order. Be prepared to run when Big Ella's potions "kick in", as you'd say,' he added softly.

'No wait!' I panicked and called out as he wafted away. 'I have something important to say to ...' I hesitated. Roc and his men had stopped talking and were looking at me expectantly. The word DOOM flashed across my eyes.

'And what is it that you have to say, my dear young lady?' asked Roc with an indulgent smile.'

Ha, I'd forgotten I was a girl. Go, girl! I fiddled with one of my woolly plaits and waved it at Roc with a girly giggle. 'I just wish to thank you, Lord Roc, and your lovely captains for being so nice to me and my big brother.'

'Awwwww,' said Roc. 'Thank you, pretty lady.'

This was going so well, I even batted my eyelids!

Shane's kick on my ankle brought me back to reality before I went completely over the top with sugary words.

'What are we going to do?' whispered Shane as I sat down.

However, other events were starting to happen.

The first loud parp came from the skinniest soldier. That was quickly followed by another and another. The hall soon filled with thundery explosions of belly wind – and the smelly pong that went with it. And then all the explosions started. At first it was just a few loud burps, but the noises spread and it was like a wind orchestra. The scared servants ran screaming from the hall – in case they'd be blamed, I supposed. The moans of the soldiers became louder and louder as they clutched their stomachs and rolled around the floor. Roc and the captains rushed over to see what was going on.

'They've had enough of Big Ella's horrid mixtures to keep them busy for a few days,' Mister Lewis's voice wafted in my ear again. 'By then Rory Rua and his men will be well prepared for them. Now, while they're busy we must go and look for the Grant. Come along, boy,' he called softly at the doorway to the kitchen stairs.

Before we could stop him, Ossie came running, his princely clothes standing out like a raspberry lolly in a snowdrift. Shane and I grabbed our bikes and ran along with Ossie towards the main stairs.

'Stop!' shouted Roc, holding his nose and pushing a groaning soldier out of his way. 'I know you, boy,' he said, pointing straight at Ossie. 'Those are the ears and wiry red hair of my cousin Rory Rua! Seize them!' he bellowed to the captains.

Ossie went to take the club from his belt, but I shouted at him. He wouldn't have a chance against this lot. We bumped our bikes down the winding stairs and headed through the castle door.

'This way,' Mister Lewis called out. Well, that wasn't any help — he was still invisible and the courtyard was pitch dark, so we couldn't see his spaceship gloves. We mounted our bikes, but it was too late.

My heart sank right down to Miss Lee's silly red shoes when I was pulled from my bike and dragged to a building on the far side of the courtyard. Behind me, Ossie and Shane were shouting, but that was just pointless. The bolt on the door was pulled back and we were pushed inside. Our bikes were thrown in after us.

'Now,' snarled Roc through the bars. 'You will rot here for trying to outwit Lord Roc. As for you, my dear Osgur,' he sneered at the kid. 'You will be held for ransom and I shall have your father's castle, which I've always coveted. Ha!' He laughed. 'I think he will oblige because, if he does not, you, will die along with those other fools. Guard them,' he barked at two of his men. 'We shall be back to deal with all of them shortly.'

We could hear him and his captains laughing as they went back to the castle.

'It's OK, Ossie,' I said to the kid as I turned on my bicycle lamp. 'Mister Lewis will be along shortly, and he'll sort everything.'

'Eh,' said a quiet voice behind us,

'Mister Lewis!' I exclaimed.' Why are you in here?'

'I'm afraid I sort of slipped in with you all,' he muttered, returning to his complete self.

'Well, can you slip out again and get us out of here?' asked Shane. 'We've got to find the Grant or we'll all be up the creek.'

'I'm afraid I can't do that,' Mister Lewis said apologetically. 'Apart from ancient portals, I can't waft through locked doors.'

Oh great! I could almost feel the grim reaper coming for Shane and me, and imagined the two of us in an afterlife of wafting about with Mister Lewis and Ossie. I took a really deep breath to hold off panicking. 'What's that smell?' I sniffed.

'You mean the stink from the castle?' said Shane.

'No,' put in Ossie. 'Milo is right. It's a sweet, fruity odour.'

I took another deep sniff. 'I know that lemony smell!' I cried. 'Remember that time we cycled to the stony wasteland, Shane, when we were looking for Miss Lee, and we got that smell? This is it! This is the place! Look!' I cried as I swept my bicycle lamp around. 'It's exactly the same shape!'

The lemony smell was coming from a dark corner.

'Shine a lamp over there,' said Mister Lewis.

Shane and I gasped at what the light showed: lying on some dirty sacks was Miss Lee. Her eyes were closed, and on her feet was a pair of very mucky boots. Her handbag was open on the floor, her stuff scattered all around her. Mister Lewis was shaking his head sadly, looking at the mess as we went towards her.

'They must have found the Grant,' said the spook, as he examined everything before putting them back in the bag. 'This is not good, not good at all. The town is doomed. We're all doomed.'

'And what about me?' asked Ossie. 'What about my family?'

'Your family would have nothing – no castle, and no lands – you'd be broke and probably have to live on a small farm on an island off the coast of Ireland.'

'What about Miss Lee?' I put in. 'What's wrong with her?'

Mister Lewis sniffed again. 'Ah, I know now what that smell is. She has been given an ancient sleep potion disguised with lemon juice. She won't remember any of this – if we all get away from here, that is,' he added gloomily

I looked at Miss Lee's muddy boots and thought that, when she woke up she'd be devastated about losing the Grant, and she'd be embarrassed by the muddy boots. Well actually, to tell the truth, my feet were aching from those darned red shoes, so I slipped off her boots and put her red high heels beside her feet. At least she'd feel a bit better in her nice shoes.

Shane and I jumped when we heard voices out in the courtyard. Angry voices and clanking chains.

'They're going to chain us to the wall to rot!' exclaimed Ossie.

'Stay well back from the door,' said Mister Lewis. 'I'll try to scare them away. You try to wake the lady.'

Shane picked up one of Miss Lee's boots.

'What are you going to do with that?' I hissed.

'I'm going to put my arm inside it and clobber the first guy who comes in,' he hissed back.

'Yeah,' I scoffed. 'Like, you'll knock out Roc and his gang with a wellie? Give it here.'

I put the first boot on, rolling my trouser leg over it so that Miss Lee wouldn't notice. Then, when I tried to get my other foot into the second boot, something blocked it. I fished it out. It was a folded document, yellow with age.

Carefully, Mister Lewis took the paper from me and unfolded it, holding it under my bike lamp.

'The Grant!' he exclaimed. 'She had the Grant in her boot all the time! The clever lady. Oh, dear, oh dear,' he sighed. 'If only we had found it earlier.' Then he groaned. 'It's too late now. Much too late.'

My heart sank even more when we heard the shouts and the clanking chains coming closer.

'What will you do with the Grant, Mister Lewis?' I whispered.

He shrugged his shoulders and then handed it to Ossie.

'You are Roc's kin, boy,' he sighed. 'He might spare you. Quickly, put this inside your tunic.'

Now Roc and his men were coming

even closer, shouting and rattling the keys to scare us – which he did, ignoring Mister Lewis's ghostly moans, which sounded like a cat with a furball. Well, let's face it, Mister Lewis was nervous for all of us. He knew what it was like to be dead.

Ossie stared at the document for a moment and then raced across to where Miss Lee was sleeping.

'What are you doing?' I hissed as he placed the Grant in Miss Lee's hands.

'Trust me,' he whispered.

The key was now turning in the lock.

'Caught like rats,' Roc sneered through the bars. 'And now you'll die like rats. Listen to the chains, people. They will be with you until your eyes fall out and your bones rot.'

Just then, Miss Lee began to stir in her sleep. She stretched her arms and looked at the Grant on her lap. Still drowsy and confused, she lifted it up and, as she did so, everything started to change. The air around us shimmered and the walls went out of focus. It was that same sinking feeling as in the woods earlier. Mister Lewis looked around, his face beaming. 'This is it!' he whispered. '*This* is the third portal. Somehow Ossie's contact with Miss Lee has opened it. You're on your way home, boys, you and the nice lady.'

'Oh, my goodness,' said our teacher, taking a deep breath. 'Have I been asleep?'

She rubbed her eyes, and the faces of the soldiers at the window faded, the last one being the angry scowl of Roc.

'Loser!' I hissed.

My bicycle torch spluttered and went out, and so did Mister Lewis. He simply disappeared, along with Ossie.

Morning was breaking. The prison had returned to the shambles we knew. The lock on the door lay open on the ground. Miss Lee gradually came to her senses and realised that me and Shane were there.

'What are you two boys doing in this forsaken place? More to the point,' she continued as she looked around with a dazed expression. 'What am I doing here?' She gazed at me and added, 'Milo, is that a ... wig and a dress you are wearing?'

To distract her, Shane said quickly, 'We were looking for you, Miss. Everyone is looking for you.'

Miss Lee shook her head, like a dog shaking off water.

While Miss Lee was still trying to work out what had happened to her, I whipped the wig off my head and stuffed it in my pocket, tucking the dress into my jeans at the same time, so it looked more like a shirt.

'Ah! I'm starting to remember,' Miss Lee exclaimed. 'Those two brats, Wedge and whatsit! I think I was doing research around here and found them emptying a sack of tin mugs. I told them those antiques are part of our heritage and should be handed over to the museum, but they just ran off. Funny thing, though,' she said with a puzzled frown. 'The door seemed to slam shut itself. Those two nitwits had already run away.'

'Maybe it was the wind,' said Shane. 'One of those sorta little whirlwind ones.'

'Perhaps,' said Miss Lee, still looking puzzled. 'Anyway, I must have have fallen asleep. I had the weirdest dreams,' she went on. 'I'm glad you two heroes came to find me. 'Let's get out of here.'

Then she stood up and looked down at her feet. 'Glory be!' she yelped. 'Those two must have pinched my boots. And just look at the state of my shoes!'

CHAPTER TWENTY-ONE

OSSIE'S BIG DAY

'**N**eat gear,' Shane whispered in my ear. 'Very macho, Milo. Perfect for scaring young kids and old ladies. Mind that hair doesn't stab someone.'

Well, maybe I had overdone the hair gel, but the T-shirt with the image of a snarling medieval knight swinging a sword was pure class.

Shane, on the other hand, was wearing a long yellow shirt with a leather belt and knee-length green shorts.

'You look like apple and custard.' I grinned back at him.

'Perfect,' he said. 'A classy dessert, that's me!'

The noisy, crowded courtyard was alive with knights – some of them on horseback. There were soldiers with lances; swordsmen mock fighting; lowly peasants; and a few baldy monks. Most of the women were wearing long velvety dresses and pointy hats which had bits of lace hanging from them. Others wore the sort of peasant clothes you'd see in history books about hard times.

No, we hadn't been whooshed back to the fourteen hundreds again; it was the opening day of the castle, and the whole place was buzzing. We walked among the chattering crowd, and we really wished we could tell them that we were responsible for all this jollity.

'What's the point of being brilliant heroes if we can't be famous?' Shane moaned.

'Who'd believe us?' I said. 'We'd be jeered as nutters for the rest of our lives.'

'We believe you,' a voice whispered, and spaceship gloves patted our faces.

'Mister Lewis!' I cried. 'You're here!'

'I am indeed,' he declared as he materialised. 'And Ossie. Come, lad,' he whispered. 'You'll fit in very well.'

We cheered when Ossie suddenly materialised with a big grin – still wearing my blue cycle helmet

'My old home,' he said. 'Cold!'

'I think you mean *cool*,' I said, laughing. 'Come on, let's have a look around.'

'I'm not exactly dressed for the occasion,' said Mister Lewis.

'Nobody will notice,' said Shane. 'Look around, there are all kinds of weird costumes. Chill, man.'

'Just try to keep your feet on the ground,' I added. 'No wafting.'

The jollity was pure manic as we strolled around. Down near the portcullis there was an archery competition.

'Ah,' said Shane. 'Let's have a go, lads. There will be a prize.'

Well, he shot his arrow over the target and hit the back wall. My effort just fell to the ground.

'Go on, lad,' Mister Lewis urged Ossie. 'Show them how it's done.'

Ossie picked up the bow like a pro. He stood erect, aimed, and shot a straight bullseye. The crowd clapped. He took another arrow and sliced it through the first one. The crowd cheered. And when he shot the third arrow through the other two, everyone went mad, clapping and cheering.

'Wow!' said the man in charge. 'You've rightly won the top prize.' He handed Ossie one of those cheap trophies you'd get in knick-knack shops. 'Nice wig,' he went on, pointing to Ossie's long, red hair. 'Very authentic. Good girl.'

I tensed, waiting for Ossie's outburst, but luckily two men lifted him up for all to see and cheer again and again.

'A precious silver bowl,' Ossie cried, holding it up as if it was the most magnificent thing ever. 'I wish my archery tutor could see this,' he shouted, which raised a loud laugh from the crowd.

As we all made our way across the courtyard, Mister Lewis and Ossie were lagging behind, everybody was oohing and aahing over the trophy, congratulating the little archer. Shane and I were passing the arch of the portcullis, with its KEEP OUT sign, when two figures in black medieval peasant gear jumped out from a dark recess. Wedge and Crunch. Just what we needed – NOT!

Wedge grinned as the two of them pushed us farther into the arch. 'Look who it is, the nerdiest nerds in town. Got your pocket money, guys?'

Of course we tried to push them away when they went to search our pockets, but their bony fingers were well versed in pinching flesh – especially lots of flesh like Shane's. As Ossie passed close to the arch Shane shouted out to him to get Mister Lewis.

Our hearts sank when Ossie came on through, still carrying his trophy and told us Mister Lewis had gone ahead to see Big Ella in the food tent. Crunch roughly pushed me into Wedge's iron clutches and turned his mean eyes on Ossie.

'Hello there,' he said with a nasty grin. 'Nice piece of tin you have there, sweetheart. That'll go nicely with our collection. What do you think, Crunch?'

Crunch let go of Shane's yellow shirt and pushed him towards me.

'Ooh ah,' he smiled. 'Bit of class, that. It should melt nicely with the rest of our stuff, Wedge.'

Ossie frowned as the bully boys were pushing me and Shane around. But as they moved towards him and he saw their faces in daylight, he went totally mental.

'Thieves!' he shouted. 'Did I not already set you running – and now you come back for more? Fools!'

'Huh?' grunted Wedge, who had no idea

what Ossie was shouting about. The two bullies paused for second, and then they both laughed. First big mistake. To me and Shane they were Wedge and Crunch, but to Ossie they were the medieval forebears who'd tried to nick our bikes in the past.

'Calm down, little girl,' said Crunch, laughing.

Oops, second big mistake!

Before we could even think what to do next, Ossie put down his trophy and, with flying kicks and trained, lightning fists, he had our arch enemies screaming for help.

'I ... am ... not ... a ... girl!' he roared, picking up his trophy.

Shane looked back at the two dazed victims. 'Careful, guys,' he warned as he stepped over Crunch and Wedge. 'This kid has a whole history of neat moves.'

'And he's our oldest friend,' I put in.

Mister Lewis was sitting at Big Ella's table in the marquee, eyeing the goodies and wondering what to do with the straw in his glass of juice. Sitting on another seat, chatting to Mister Lewis was Miss Lee.

'Ah, my heroes,' she said. Then she looked curiously at Ossie. I got ready to jump in if she mentioned the 'girl' word, but they just stared at one another.

'My goodness,' laughed Big Ella looking from one to the other. 'Two identical redheads at my table.'

'Are you from around here?' Miss Lee asked Ossie.

'Just visiting,' I put in.

'From Afar,' Shane giggled.

'Ah,' said Miss Lee. 'I'm admiring how your medieval clothes go so well with the blue cycle helmet. What a funny coincidence,' she said, turning to the rest of us, 'I'm descended from Rory Rua's famous son. He was nicknamed Osgur of the Blue Headgear.'

'We know, Miss,' I butted in. 'He raised the alarm when his father's castle was about to be captured by a kinsman of his. Me and Shane do our research just like you tell us. It's all on Google.'

'Yes! Google Earth, that's me,' Ossie said with a huge grin.

'This is all very interesting,' interrupted Shane. 'But we're wasting good eating time. Are you ever going to cut that cream cake, Gran?'

MILO AND ONE DEAD ANGRY DRUID

When Shane's gran digs up a weird ancient stone, best buddies Milo and Shane find themselves face to face with its owner — one dead angry druid. Willie Jones's lizard goes mental and Shane disappears. Milo is in deep, deep trouble and he needs a rescue plan before midnight strikes.

MILO AND THE LONG LOST WARRIORS

Milo and his best buddy Shane are on a school trip to a museum and a mock battle. So far, so cool.

Milo's ghostly friend Mister Lewis wants to help three lost warriors who are trapped in the museum. They're from the real Battle of Clontarf, one thousand years ago.

But then the two school bullies, Crunch and Wedge, turn up, and they're just looking for trouble …